Rag Duck

Written by Hatty Skinner
Illustrated by Louise Anglicas

Collins

Get socks and rags.

Cut up the socks.

Cut the top.

Pack in the rags.

Tuck it up.

Pad the red sock.

Pin on the red sock.

a pen
dots
rags

It is a duck!

Mum has a rod.

The duck can hop!

Mum has a red hat.

/r/

After reading

Letters and Sounds: Phase 2
Word count: 54
Focus phonemes: /g/ /o/ /c/ ck /e/ /u/ /r/ /h/
Common exception words: the, is, and, has
Curriculum links: Expressive arts and design
Early learning goals: Reading: read and understand simple sentences; use phonic knowledge to decode regular words and read them aloud accurately; read some irregular words

Developing fluency

- Your child may enjoy hearing you read the book.
- Take turns to read a page but encourage your child to read all the labels, too.

Phonic practice

- On pages 2–3, ask your child to find the word with the /r/ sound, and to sound out and blend the word. (r/a/g/s – **rags**)
- On pages 4–5, ask them to find a word that has the /e/ sound. (*red*) Next, ask them to find the word that has the /u/ sound. (*cut*)
- On page 4, can they find two spellings for the /c/ sound? If necessary support them by pointing to **Cut** and **sock**.
- Look at the "I spy sounds" pages (14–15). Point to the rod and say: I spy an /r/ in rod. Challenge your child to point to and name different things they can see that begin with the /r/ sound. (e.g. *rag duck*, *rain*, *rainbow*, *rabbit*, *rat*, *ruler*, *rags*) Point to the crayons and say: I spy an /r/ in this word. Am I right? Encourage your child to say crayon and listen for the /r/ sound.

Extending vocabulary

- Turn to page 3 and discuss the meaning of **rip**. Ask your child what things can rip. (e.g. *paper*, *rags*) Ask: Are there other words that could be used instead? (e.g. *tear*, *pull apart*)